The
Anecdotal II

William Bateman

authorHOUSE®

AuthorHouse™
1663 Liberty Drive
Bloomington, IN 47403
www.authorhouse.com
Phone: 1 (800) 839-8640

This is a work of fiction. All of the characters, names, incidents, organizations, and dialogue
in this novel are either the products of the author's imagination or are used fictitiously.

Published by AuthorHouse 04/04/2019

ISBN: 978-1-5462-5543-7 (sc)
ISBN: 978-1-5462-5542-0 (e)

Print information available on the last page.

This book is printed on acid-free paper.

CONTENTS

"A TRUE STORY"

My mother, a woman of exacts, was born on a Chippewa Indian Reservation, 1911 to her mother Ida and a Chippewa brave.

They lived on the Reservation until my mother was five years old, And then the Native American packed his family up, and moved all the Way from the Seattle, Washington area, across the country to New York State, and to a town, where there was an Indian reservation.

After establishing his family on the reservation, he went into the City and opened up a furniture moving business.

Soon, the business was thriving, and becoming a popular small Business.

But, One day, after being in their location long enough to be Making a pretty good income, while moving a particularly heavy piece Of furniture, there was a very serious accident.

Ida's husband was killed, when a thick and cumbersome piece of Furniture fell on him and crushed him.

After the funeral, Ida made it plain that she wouldn't be marrying Another brave. She was almost immediately moved off the Reservation, and She, with her daughter, left New York State and Moved to Newark, New Jersey.

Where Ida met, and married a black man named James Johnson. Who proved to be a hard taskmaster, so! No doubt, it was a contentious Union, but Ida put up with it, staying married until her death in about 1917. By then her daughter Martha had met and was on the verge of Marrying the coming young suitor, named William Bateman. The next year, they were married, and moved into their own Apartment, away from her hard-timing step-father.

Mr. Johnson, never forgot or forgave my mother for not acting More like a daughter and (I guess) mainly, for not taking his last Name. Whenever she signed anything, the last name was always Dubrey, instead of Johnson.

Martha, Ida's daughter, had been going to school in New York State, and when they moved to Newark, NJ, Ida had all of her Daughter's papers dealing with school, Transferred to a school in Newark, N.J.

And Martha began school, in schools that either had very few Black students, or no black students at all. In this environment, she seemed to thrive, and saw herself as Being the only black girl in her classes, as more of a challenge and Seemed to show abilities that black children didn't usually show.

From her years in grammar school, Junior High School, and High School, she showed a marked ability, to end her school years by Graduating Com Laudi, (Second in Excellence, in the entire school).

Not because her grades put her there, only because she Was black, and could not graduate with the highest honors Of Valedictorian, in an, all-white school.

She took on different jobs after Highs school. Opting not to go to College, she met my father, William Bateman, fell in-love with him, and After a somewhat lengthy courtship, they married.

During the marriage, they had five children, four boys, and one Girl. The children's names were, Walter (Buddie), William Jr. (Willie), Charles Robert (chuck), Carol Ann, and John David Bateman.

She raised her children within the tenets of her up-bringing. She Did not have any of them baptized into her husband's religion, which Was Baptist, but! He didn't go to church that much anyway.

And even though the kids went to a Baptist Church, they were Not baptized. They all ended up joining their own religious groups.

In the end Walter, became Muslim, William, became Catholic, Charles & Carol became, Buddhist, John became a Methodist preacher.

All of her children ended up being someone of note, in His and her Community in this great Society Of success and failure.

Both my mother, and my father, died early, my father died at the Age of 45, my mother at the age of 52.

I never got to go to my father's funeral because, I was overseas, And couldn't get back to the States in time. But, I got to go to my Mother's funeral, when I was stationed in Japan. It took me 16 Hrs. to Get home that time. I was bumping all kinds of people off of their Flights to get there.

But, the fact is, that no-matter how us kids strayed from our Teachings, we always seemed to land on our feet.

Walter died an honored member of the cities fathers. Carol died' An artist, and a well-known member of the art community, John died, a Retired educator and Athlete, who taught at a local High School, both Track & Field, and Mentoring, plus teaching tenth grade students.

Charles is a retired Teacher of English, and some other courses, And is still teaching in his spare time, although, he will probably end Up being a teacher all of his life.

And me? Willie! I retired from Federal Service with 37yrs. 21 of those Years in the USAF, and the rest, working on shipyards, and assorted Jobs.

And! I've written two novels, Welcome Home our Heroes. A Fictional novel about the sixties, and the fight for the rights of a Returned Viet Nam hero, whether he would not, or whether he would Be buried in the town's tomb of War Hero's.

And Guerrero, A four book saga, about my ex-wife's grand-father. Who rode with Pancho Villa during the Mexican Revolution, at the age Of thirteen.

So! You see! None of us Bateman's were anything less than we Could possibly be, and, who knows, When I close my eyes for the last Time on this planet, I may end up with my family once again, who Knows?!!!

THE END

A MODERN HERCULES

When I was a young teenager, every once and a while, I would stop by my dad's job, and watch him work.

And you must remember, the time of the occurrence was back in the early forties. Back during the time when-everyone was working for the IIWW effort.

My dad worked in a auto shop called Belmont Auto Springs. Where they actually forged springs for cars and trucks.

Many times I would stand and watch him work the forge, handling white hot steel with tongs, as he curled and bent the softened steel to whatever shape he wished.

The Saturday of the occurrence, I had decided to stop by my dad's job and watch him work. Well! That day became a very scary day for me because, dad was working under an ammo truck, when suddenly one of the jacks slipped, and flew away from the truck.

And one corner of the truck came crashing down to the ground with a mighty crash, sealing my dad under that corner of the truck.

I'm sure the crash could be heard for blocks away. And it happened so quick, that everybody who was there, was stunned! surprised, and frighten.

It all happened so quickly, that no one moved at first. Instead of someone calling the police, and fire Department. there was women screaming, men yelling, and everyone running around not really helping the situation.

Someone must have called the fire Department, Because, they showed up, with the police from the thirteenth Precinct, in the 3rd Ward Newark, not far behind.

A crowd had grown, as the curious began gathering to see what was going on. As the police pushed the crowd back from the area surrounding the truck, a loud cry came from the crowd, and I glance to where one of the onlookers was pointing.

The end of the truck that had crashed to the ground, began to slowly move upward.

The whole crowd seemed to hold their breath, as the end began inching up. Soon I saw my father's hand come into view.

Soon there was a loud cheer, as the end of the truck moved up more and the muscular arms and hands of my dad appeared to be holding up the fallen end of the truck.

A policeman and a fireman, rushed over to where the end of the truck was well off of the ground.

My dad told them what kind of jack to put under the end, to hold it up until he could safely crawl out from under the truck.

One of the men who worked with my dad ran into the shop and emerged with a very long jack which he placed on the ground under the area my dad was holding up with his hands.

And began jacking the end up, enough for my father to relax and crawl out from under the truck.

A mighty roar went up from the crowd once my dad was standing on his feet. He walked over to the ambulance that had also arrived, and sitting on the bumper he got his scrapes and scratches tended to.

Standing only 5'5" in height, but weighing about 195 lbs, having 25" Biceps, a 42" chest and a waistline 35" and hands that were very large, his strength that of many men that day, he was truly something to behold.

But! Then you must understand, this was just a regular day, {back in the day), and believe me! it really happened.

THE END

"A SECOND CHANCE"

When I returned to the States from Viet Nam and Thailand in 1964, little did I know, that I would make the journey though briefly, to the other-side.

Tomorrow is 20 August 2015, My Birthday. By all that's right, I shouldn't even be here to celebrate that birthday, but! Here I am! Given the gift of a second chance at life.

The beginning of my journey happened about a week back from Viet Nam & Thailand. I was stationed at Fairchild AFB, Washington State.

This one night, I wasn't feeling quite up to snuff, so I decided to hang around the barracks. But found that the longer I laid in bed, the harder it was for me to get up.

Pretty soon, I was feeling like I was going to die and I couldn't make it on my own steam. The last time I finally dragged myself from that bunk, I was literally crawling down the stairs.

I finally made it to the CQ's (Charge of Quarters) desk, and told him that I wasn't feeling good and would He call the Base Hospital, and tell them to send a vehicle to pick me up and take me there.

The CQ, not knowing what to do in this type of situation, faltered and let precious moments slip by as he stalled.

Finally a voice came from the television viewing area of the day room,

"Hell! I'll take Him to the hospital." And a young man walked over to the CQ's desk, took me by the arm and guided me, out of the barracks to where his car was parked.

After getting me into his car, he hurried around and got in the driver's side and took off. Shortly after that we arrived to the hospital. By that time, I was throwing up and I couldn't walk, and had to be helped into the Hospital.

Once inside the hospital, and a cursory examination, the doctor (who was annoyed that he had been awaken handed the guy that had drove me there a bottle of medicine saying, "Here! See that he takes this and bring him back on sick-call in the morning."

It was about one-thirty in the morning, The young black Airman backed up saying, "No! Doc! There's something really wrong with this guy, and I don't want him dying on me. No! He's your responsibility now!"

And he walked out of the hospital' Leaving me there, and they had to give me a bed until they could examine me and make a diagnosis.

I was given a bed, and after they examined me, they found that I had a life threatening ailment, they sent for my squadron commander.

I lay there barely breathing, watching as my squadron commander and the doctor talked to each other. Suddenly, there was blackness, and then was up in the far corner of the room, looking down on the whole room.

The doctor and my Squadron Commander had not moved, and were still at the foot of the bed talking. I was laying in the bed motionless, and yet, I was perched up in the far corner of the room looking at the whole scene.

Then, there was darkness and when I opened my eyes again, I was being wheeled into the operating room. I looked Around wildly and said, to the closest person beside my gurney "What are you doing, where are you taking me?"

He answered, not looking at me, "To the operating room." I said, as though that explained everything," Oh!" and passed-out again.

When I woke up again, I was in the bed with all sorts of tubes in and through me.

I was told that nine doctor's worked on my body. I had gone from a healthy 153 lbs. to 112 lbs. in two days but, thanks be to god, I prevailed and after a month of being hooked up to machines and tubes, and IV's, and a return to a weight that was to bring me completely back to a more normal healthy person.

I spent a month in the base hospital and soon gained back Most of my weight. But! I would never be the same.

Within a week after I was out of the hospital, I was back on duty. I was well for the rest of that year, as I slowly regained my health but, during that time, I slowly but surely was losing my blood count.

My blood was actually turning pink and right away, they put me back into the hospital where I stayed for three months this time.

When my blood was finally its normal color, and I was feeling normal, they finally released me back to my squadron.

From the moment I left the hospital in 1965, until today, I have never again been inside a hospital for anything except one-more operation in 2003, When I went into the hospital to have my prostate gland removed because it had cancerous cells on it.

That was the last time I was in the Hospital and now, I only go to the hospital for a physical checkup, and medication.

Today is my birthday! I'm now 82 years old, and people still take me to be in my sixties, so! You figure it out!

The End

THE PILL

WWI
1917-1918

My name is Albert Augustus Simms, and from the age of ten, I was living in an orphanage in Newark, New Jersey. My mother died in another state and I had no father to tell of, at-least my mother never spoke of one, and whenever I tried to bring one up, she'd shush me.

My grandmother left me on the steps of an orphanage with a note, explaining that, because of her age, she couldn't take care of me anymore, but didn't want to just leave me on the mean streets of the city to fend for myself.

My mother's name was Althea Alexis Simms, she was beautiful and gentle, and when I was about five years old, she would sit me on her lap and read to me from Grimm's and Anderson Fairy Tales.

Those were magical moments, and I felt warm, safe and protected listening to her soft voice bring the pages alive in my minds-eye. I always remember those moments, and how the soft perfume she used, was always in the air.

I recalled she did house work for a rich white woman named Mrs. Wockman.

She had an Extra job taking in ironing, from all of the working people living in the same apartment building we did on weekends, for a fee.

My mother got extra clothes for me from Mrs. Wockman, and those were the clothes I wore to school.

When she got laid off of her job at Mrs. Wockman's, and most of the people who had hired her to iron their clothes, moved away, Died or whatever, hard times set in as she ran around trying to find another job.

We finally had to move to her mother's house, and stayed there while she tried to get a new job. When she was offered a job out of state, she decided to leave me with her mother because, she only had enough for one fare, and although I could ride for free, she didn't have enough food she only had enough for herself but, while she was gone, she died.

When my grandmother realized that she couldn't take care of me because of her age, she took me to an orphanage and left me there.

The first years were the hardest because, I was about seven sitting there on the steps of that orphanage. I can remember the resentment I felt, when my Granny left me sitting out in front of that Orphanage with a not pinned to my coat, not really knowing why she had left me there.

They found me there and took me in and for the next three Years, I had a small hope that someone would take me away from there but, My tenth year came and went but by my tenth year, I had given up as I thought to myself 'So! Who's going to adopt a ten year old black boy?' Well, as the years went by, I went to Junior High and high school, and actually graduated with honors, from both.

When I reached the age of seventeen, I was able to walk away from the orphanage and went and got a Job in a hash house washing dishe's, and lived in a small walk in-apartment. The year was 1917, and the Great war had been going on for three years or more.

Two of the boys I knew in school, dropped by my apartment to tell me that they were going to enlist in the army, and get into the fighting.

I gave them a perplexed look saying, "Why would you want to go and fight the white man's war?"

My friend named Ronald Brown said, "Look! me and Earl have been around trying to get jobs, and all they have out there is dish washing, waiters, red caps, and any job that is at the bottom of the ladder.

Well! We decided that we could do better, so, we've decided to enlist, fight the Kaiser, and save the world"

My other friend Earl Wilder said, "Why are you looking so stunned?

"Look! We went down to the recruiter, and were told that they are now recruiting blacks to fight in the trenches in Europe." I said angrily, "Huh! They run out of white boys to die For THEIR country! Over there in some foreign land, they never been to before?"

Ronnie said, "Aw man! Come on, don't think of it that way, At least we'll be seeing a different country, and we'll be getting paid to be there."

Earl said, excitement in his voice, "And we'll be seeing lots of white women."

I looked at them, barely able to keep my contempt for both of them from showing, "Yea! That's what I Thought.

You best be listening to me! They got trees over there too, with limbs just as thick as the ones we have over here. And I'm sure that those white folks don't want people like us over there, even if we are there to help defend them."

Ronnie said, "Well! Are you going to go down and enlist so that we can be together? I'd hate to leave you behind with all of these fine brown frames to yourself. Hell! You can keep an eye on earl, and keep him out of trouble if he gets too close, to any of those white gals over there."

They kept coaxing me and I finally said, "You're right about one thing, I can't just settle for the work they want to give me so, I guess I will enlist! But it's only because I don't want Earl to get lynched Because he's running around after those women over there."

Looking at Earl, I said, "The trouble with you is, that you still don't know when you got your pants on backwards. You only realize it when you have to take a leak, and there's no zipper to be found because, it is in the wrong place. So yea! It makes sense that I go along for the ride. If I stayed here, and let you guys go over there alone, I'd be worried about you all the time"

The next morning, I went down to the recruiting office, and this big strapping white boy was sitting behind a desk. His uniform freshly starched, and his cap tilted at a cocky angle on his head.

He handed me a form, a set smirk on his face, As he said," Here you go boy! Hell! You look so fit, I think you could go over there and whip the Boch!(German Soldiers) all by yourself."

I smiled and said, "Huh! I guess I'll have to, you guys Sho-Ain't-Doin such a good job these days."

The guy sitting at the table glaring angrily at me, all red in the face and said, "You trying to be funny boy?"

Before I could respond he said, "Just fill out the form and take a seat, we'll be with you in a minute."

I went back over and sat down in the section for coloreds, the place was packed, and for the next three hours, I sat there and finally, my name was called and I went over to the desk.

The guy sitting there said, "Go over there, strip to your shorts, and stand in that line near the opened door.

I went over, stripped, and stood in line, waiting to enter the room and, wondering what was behind the door. But, I found out quick enough. When I entered that room, I was examined from head to toe, And after I had redressed, I was led out and given a slip of paper.

The same guy said, "If you pass the physical then You'll be called back in. When you report, you'll be given another physical, and will be given your shots. You'll be notified to return within two weeks for the swearing in Ceremony and you'll be in the army."

When I got the call to go back and be sworn in, my two friends came along with me. We had all passed, and was Classified-1A.

We stood in a room that was half black and half white and raised our hands and took the oath of allegiance. We were now full-fledged army men, and had a date that ordered us to be at the Greyhound Bus Terminal on the following Tuesday.

We couldn't carry any luggage, but could carry a shaving kit.

When we met at the bus station, we were all put on special buses and driven to Fort Dix, New Jersey, the army camp right outside of Trenton, New Jersey.

We went through a very tough basic training, our DI was black. A tough, loud mouth, Gunnery Sergeant named Garner, James H.

He told us that we would be going to France to fight the Boch, and we should take the books he had passed out to us and learn as much French as we Could.

The one's that caught on fast could teach the others. Not Him! He said he could speak a couple of different language's French being one of them.

I guess me, Earl, and Ronnie were quick studies, because, we studied ever night and we spoke to each other all the time until we had a pretty good spin on French.

A lot of the guys were like that but, there were some who just couldn't get the language.

Gunnery Sgt. Garner put us through our paces and was always saying, "I won't have you guys going over there and acting like a bunch of no brained nigger's.

"When I finish with you, you won't think of nothing but fighting the Boch. Hell! You'll Eat Boch, Sleep Boch and in the end, you'll kill Boch.

"And I want to see every twitching asshole back here in one piece. I want you to show those white bastards that we have as much heart, and are just as tough as they are; And I'm talking about your white counterparts, who will be going with you."

I looked over at Earl and smiled, I'd have to talk to him about that later on.

That night, when we were all doing our house-keeping chores, I said to Earl,

"Look! You heard the Sarg right? We are to concentrate on the job ahead."

Earl smiled and said, "I heard him. And I didn't hear him Say that women were out of bounds. And remember, we WON'T be in Georgia, or Alabama."

I said angrily, "What's wrong with you Nigger! You got Air on the brain? We may not be in Georgia or Alabama but, you'll swear we were, if you get to messing with those women over there.

"Take my word for it, they will string you up so fast, you won't realize it until you're in hell. So! me and Ronnie are going to keep you in our sights at all times when we're behind the lines and not fighting the Boch."

After six weeks of intensive training, especially trench warfare, we were finally ready to ship out and the excitement was contagious and we were all stepping pretty good as we marched from our bus to the troop ship down in New York Harbor.

We were all standing in ranks and the Sarg said, "OK! You men! Remember my words. You are not going to France on Any damned vacation.

"You are going to fight the Boch! And if you focus on that job, you'll be far too damned busy to get into any Kind-a trouble.

Also remember, Uncle Sam is sending you there to make sure that the Boch don't come over here, where your mama's an daddies might have to fight em' on our land.

So! You go over there and give em hell."

We also got some words from our Commanding Officer but, we didn't listen because, what could a white officer tell us that the Sarg hadn't told us already?"

We were really sharp and our marching was really a groove. Like the Sarg said when we were stumbling around and didn't know how to march, "When you boys decide to stop stumbling around like a bunch eh damned sissies, I'll teach you how to march." He got us all in rows and said, "When you march for me, all I want to hear is one boot hitting the ground. Hell, don't be afraid to dig em in, that's what they gave you boots for. So! I'm telling you now, If I hear more than one boot, then every bodies got to run three miles."

Hell! We wised up real quick and in no time, we were second to the best marching unit on Fort Dix. Not only that, we became crack shots and I guess Earl, (Being Earl!) stayed in trouble of one kind or another and broke the record for peeling spuds (Potatoes), swabbing Decks, and latrine duty, He just didn't get it.

All he had to do was follow orders, which he found hard to do. Me and Ronnie were at the top of our class when it came to soldering, and were promoted to the rank of PFC (Private First Class).

The trip across the Pacific Ocean, was one that I will never forget. As soon as we found out where our bunks were located, all three of us went down and saw the ships doctor, and when Earl asked him what we could use to keep us from getting seasick.

The doctor smiled and said, I could give you some Dramamine but, instead of wasting it on three healthy specimens like you boys, I'll say this, go down to the ship store and get a couple of boxes of salteen crackers apiece. You boys keep popping those salteen's every once in a while, and you won't get sick."

Earl said skeptically, "Not one day?" The doctor said, "Not one minute, of one day!" We left sick bay, and after asking around, found the Ship Store and immediately bought up almost all of the salteen crackers and divided them up between us. All the way over, we weren't sick one minute of one day and feeling sympathy for the rest of the guys, we watched as they were sick every day and, we knew that if we had told them why we weren't getting sick, they would have probably thrown us over board. When we finally docked in Liverpool, England and had been marched off of the ship,

Right away, I could see the difference in that place and America, and began making Comparisons, The streets were smaller, the people were strange to me, and they were ALL white.

We all mounted trucks, and were driven to another Airport, from where we were flown to France.

When we landed, we were marched to this village and could actually hear bombs blowing up, and lots of yelling and screaming, somewhere in the distance from that village.

We were housed in a small armory, and weren't allowed outside at all. There was two hundred and fifty of us, and we were all black.

Earl said, "It couldn't be that these people are afraid of us or something?"

Ronnie said, "It's not that they are afraid of us, they just think we'll go native and start throwing spears at them, and shooting arrows and, you know! Climbing tree's and stuff."

We all laughed, but deep down, we all felt an anticipated fear but, we were saved from embarrassing ourselves, and perhaps everyone involved for, we shipped out right away for the front, without having had a chance to ever sample the booze or eyeball the women.

Truck after truck, loaded with us fresh troops heading for the front, some with white boys from other villages, and some with us negro's were driven for what seemed like forever, before we had to stop and refuel.

Once that was accomplished, we continued our ride. I said finally, "Exactly what the hell are we doing here?"

Earl said, "Hey Al, are you scared?" His face was sweating and his eyes were wide with the terror of The moment. He looked at me and Ronnie, saying, "Fella's! What are we gonna do"

Just about that time, we heard loud sounds of bombs going off and rifles being fired, and a whole lot of yelling.

We were led to the trenches where we stood and watch as the men charged across open ground firing as they went.

Where we were in the trench, we could also see our cannon going off sending shot across all of that barbed wire strung up all over the battle-field into the Kaiser's lines.

Suddenly, those Germans came back with answering Fire, and began knocking our men over like ten pins. When we saw our men going down, it dawned on us, that we were in the middle of a REAL war, And wasn't no newsreel in some neighborhood theater and that we could all get killed.

Earl pointed his rifle and started to fire. I stopped Him saying, "You can't shoot yet."

Earl said, "What are you doing? Get your damned Hands off of my rifle, Besides! I've got a right to fire back don't I?"

I said angrily, "Yea! You've got a right to fire back but, if you shoot now, you'll probably hit some of our men."

Well, we stayed out there in those trenches until we thought we'd go nuts because, all we'd do was charge up out of our trenches at those Germans, and then they would charge at us and this went on until they said, that we could get a break. We were loaded on trucks and sent back behind the lines where we could shower, shave, and relax for a few days.

They sent us back to that town, and that Armory not far from the fighting, where we could get some hot food, and relaxation.

When we finally ventured out of the Armory, to see what the locals were like, the people of the town looked at us with fear in their eyes and distanced themselves from us. We finally had to approach them, and very carefully show them that we weren't a threat to them or their town.

Once we broke the ice, and the townspeople realized that we weren't any kind of threat, there was music and dancing and we were all invited into their houses where we ate dinner with them.

No one in the town had ever seen a black man in the flesh and word had spread around the town that our skin was really this color and that it wouldn't wash off.

Once they found out that all of those browns of difference shades wouldn't wash off, from the darkest black to almost white, the girls came around and began mingling with us, their parents not minding at all.

The Officer in charge of us was a white Captain who was always drunk and made his headquarters in an cabaret, fondling the girls, eating, and sleeping.

So, actually, we had the run of the town for three days because, after three days, we would be going back to the front.

I found that within those three days, we actually Laid the foundation for World War II. We were all sitting in a cabaret during the second night and Earl was trying to convince one of the girls to go upstairs with him.

She said no and then she said a strange-thing. She said, "How did your skin get that color?"

25

Thinking quickly, a look of concentration, on his face, which cleared up just as quick, Earl suddenly smiled widely and said loudly, "To be truthful, we are actually white."

All he small talk in the place stopped and everyone was paying attention, as Earl looked at me and winked saying, "Well! What happened was, we were recruited for a very special mission over here, a kind of scientific experiment."

One of the young town's men in the gathering, said, "If it's not a secret, can you tell us what that mission is?" Earl said, looking around cautiously, "But you have to promise me! Not to breath a word of it to anyone.

"It's a military secret, and could get you and maybe your whole family killed if you told."

Looking around with a secretive Aire', Again he said in almost a whisper, "It all started in Washington, DC, and beings so many of us white boys were being killed on a daily basis, they asked for a lots of volunteers to go on a secret mission. It turns out that all of us volunteers were to be Guinea pigs and were given a pill. Now!

This was an Extra-ordinary pill because, it turned us dark and it even affected our hair by giving us short tight curls.

They gave us the name of night fighters and that's when we are at our best, for we only fight at night when the Boch can't see us, as long as we squint our eyes and don't smile."

The girl he was trying to convince to go upstairs with him said, "But suppose some of us get pregnant? Would Our babies, be this color?"

Earl gave her a reassuring grin, saying, "Ahh! But! You haven't heard the best part.

"This skin-color only last's for a year, just about the time we are due to rotate back to the States. Once we get home, this color will fade and we'll Once again be white."

At first the people were still somewhat skeptic's until the last instant and one of them said,"Once and a while we have movies from the western world that show people like you, you're telling me that all of those people are basically white?"

Without even batting his eyes Earl said, "Ahh! Now those folks had to get a shot, a pill is only temporary, if they get a shot? "Then they stay that color forever!

"Now us?" Pointing at himself and us, he said, "Now we just want it for this war, but! Hell! We don't intend to Stay! This way forever."

The people were sold, and you could see them relax completely. They were all now more friendly toward us once back on the lines, while we were back in the trenches, fearing the next charge that we were to be a part of I said, "Earl! What's going to happen when those people find out that you were lying to them?"

Earl shrugged saying, "Huh! By then we'll be long gone from this place and besides, how will they find out that I was lying? All of us are back here on the lines."

I said, "But suppose the Captain finds out what's going on, and reports us to Headquarters Earl said "Hell! He's always so high, crying in his beer about being brought low by

Headquarters, by being assigned to a troop of niggers, he's too busy feeling sorry for himself so! I figure that the only time he's sober is when we're up here on the lines so that he won't get his butt shot off."

Laughing to himself, Earl continued by saying, "Don't you worry! They won't find out, Trust me!"

Ronnie said angrily, "Trust YOU? Yea! And don't worry, They WILL! Find out. You wait until all of those Black-Ass-babie's Start popping up. And when the color doesn't fade and they realize that they had been conned, there's gonna be hell to pay."

Earl laughed saying, "What are they going to do? Shoot us?"

Ronnie said, "If they can track us down? You're damned right, they would kill us in a heartbeat. Especially! If we do something against orders."

Earl said, laughing with bitter/sweet irony. "Track Us down? Huh! You seem to forget, to them, we all look alike. Besides, I doubt if they would take the time to look for us."

Well, in the end, all three of us survived the trenches, Ronnie losing a leg, and Earl, getting shot in the butt, and me? I got winged a few times but managed to survive with a few bullet wounds but we actually killed a few of the Boch, and came away from that war with us all getting promotions to corporal.

Ronnie went on to become a Red Cap on the Hudson & Pacific out of Philadelphia, PA. His time in the service giving him veteran status. He was fitted with a false leg, and given that position.

Earl became the manager of a store in the black neighborhood in Newark and by making a deal with a well Established white man, in need of financial backing from a black man of influence, in order to open a clothing store on some of Earl's property, in Newark's all black 3rd ward.

But! Then, that was Earl, forever looking for a deal, and always finding a way to succeed.

Me? I went back to school and graduated from NYU in New York, and then I went to a University up in New York State. After Graduating, I married a very beautiful young lady named Margie Beckworth.

We settled in DC, and began talking over me getting into politics, first I became a page, which was very hard to do but, I did it. And even though Washington, DC was 60% Black, and believe me in Washington, DC. Being black, and in the Nation's Capital, it was even harder to become a page but, through all of the bad times I faced, I came through it all and kept my eye on the prize, and worked my way up to being the best damned Democratic Senator I could possibly be.

All of us guys stayed in touch and we all married, and by my being in Government, I heard things all the time and when I got the word that over in France, there had been an incident in a small town near Florence, the incident being the multiple births of black babyies, to many of the white girls there. Instantly! I knew what it was all about. I quickly got in touch with the guy's, and we met and Had lunch to discuss it.

Ronnie said, Giving Earl a baleful glare, "OK Smart-Ass! What do we do now? You and your damned pill story."

Earl laughed saying, "It worked didn't it? Beside, white folks been getting over on us since time began, I think, a little pay back was in order; and it couldn't have come at a better time." Glaring at us; the first and only time I ever saw him serious, He said, "Who put their lives on the line so that Americans could keep on living their lives in safety?

We did! Who got shot in the ass? Who lost a leg? Who got all shot up? We did! We did this so that they could appreciate us for going to THEIR war, and defending THEIR cause, only to be treated even worse (when we got back to the States) than we had been treated before we left. Besides, almost 45 years have passed and I guess it must have leaked out of the town. But, what can we do about It Now?"

I said, "In the end, we're all a part of this because, I'm sure we left someone behind in that town.

But! Perhaps one day, we'll wonder about those kids we left behind, and perhaps realize that they have an even harder row to hoe than even we do.

I think that if the rest of the unit we were with Had found out, they would have something to say but, hell! We are all scattered to hell and beyond. All we can do Is pray that something good comes out of this.

Well! I don't know if the pill had any bearing but, when WWII came into being, and one of my two sons joined the Marines, I didn't connect that war with anything accept what was going on at the time but, when it was all over, and I was well into my forties, and the truth about Hitler's atrocities were bared to the world, how he was trying to make the white race pure, I sat back in my easy chair and chuckled to myself.

———ɯɯ———

Well! Earl and Ronnie are both gone, Earl from cancer, and Ronnie from a massive stroke, and I am the only one left alive with the story about the pill.

I thought whimsically to myself, "Maybe by now they have a pill that will make me young again, and who knows, maybe even white."

Margie, my wife of fifty-three years came into the room wondering aloud if I was having an attack of some kind or something, I was laughing so hard.

I said, "Honey! You probably wouldn't believe me If I told You!"

THE END

"CHANGE OF STATION"

On my return to the USA from three years in Japan, in 1957, I felt like I owned the world.

I had returned to the United States with a Japanese wife, And an Ego twice the size of my body.

When our ship docked in San Diego harbor, and after what Might have been a harrowing ten days on the Pacific Ocean, Had it not been for the fact that I (Having never been on the Ocean before, except going to Coney Island, and other sea Resorts), didn't know what to expect, and knew about sea-Sickness only through movies and TV, came up with an idea.

I went to sickbay and asked the medic there, what I Needed to keep from being seasick.

He said that instead of taking medication for seasickness, I should go to the ship's Gee-dunk (store), and buy a box of Salteen Crackers, and eat one or two to keep my stomach Settled.

I went and bought all the Salteen Crackers they had and Stashed them in my duffle-bag, only keeping out one box at a Time. I never got sea-sick one minute of one day.

But! Like so many young men of that period, (And of all Periods to come), I was so self-centered, that I didn't share Them, even with my wife or anyone.

When we finally docked in San Diego, We caught a train That took us across country to New York. We then boarded a Train that took us to Newark, NJ. Where a few members of my Family met us and drove us to the house on Livingston, St.

Our stay in New Jersey was almost marred by the receipt Of my orders to proceed (After my leave was up, to an Air Station in Michigan.

My brother Buddie was at home the same time (On Leave From the Army) and he advices me to go to Washington, DC. in Order to get that changed.

He said, because of the change in my marital status, I Couldn't be Station at an isolated base.

But! I would have to physically go to DC, in order to change that. So! We planned out a trip to Washington, DC. And man! What a trip it was.

After making some phone-calls, we finally found out where I had to go, to have my Station changed to one where my wife Could accompany me.

When we arrived in Washington, DC, to me, the steady Stream of people coming and going about their business wasExciting.

I hailed a taxi, and I'm sure he knew that we were new to Washington, DC. And when I asked him where we could find a Hotel close to the Offices I had to go to, he said right away,

"The Dunbar Hotel! Would be a wise choice, because it is Close to where you need to go."

When we reached our destination, we paid off the cab Driver and he helped us unload our luggage on the steps of The Dunbar Hotel.

Going inside, with the help of a hotel worker, we managed To get our luggage up to the desk.

I signed us into the hotel, and along with a bell-hop, we Made our way up to a room.

On our way to our room, we saw the halls where cluttered With all kinds of people, who were lounging, and women of the Night were openly plying their trade.

Right away, we knew that we had made the wrong choice, But I figured that it was to-late, and that we would have face One hell-of-a-night.

We locked our luggage up inside the room, and went back Outside to see if we could find a decent place to eat dinner.

Standing on the stoop, I saw the taxi that had brought us There pull in and Park.

The driver got out and hurried up to where we were Standing. He said, "You checked in already right?"

We both nodded yes, and he thought to himself for a Moment, shrugged his shoulders, and said," Well! I can fix This so! Go up to your room and get your luggage, I'll fix it With the desk clerk."

When we returned to the front desk with our luggage, He took the luggage my wife was carrying and said quickly, "Follow me."

He led us to his taxi, and opened the cabs trunk, where we Placed our luggage.

We got into the taxi, not knowing where this man was Taking us, and somewhat hesitant about how forward he was After he had taken control of the situation.

He drove us away from that hotel, and that area. He drove To a completely different neighborhood and parked in front of A big house.

He got out and after helping my wife out of the cab, he led Us up the stairs, and into the house.

His wife met us by the door and he called a few of his kids And we introduced ourselves to everyone and his wife sat us Down at their kitchen table, and fed us.

The taxi driver said, "I have to get back to work but, I'll Talk to you again tomorrow morning. In the mean-time, my Wife and kids can take good care of you."

Before I could say anything, he was gone, and his wife was Herding us up the stairs, and into a bedroom. Where we almost Immediately fell asleep.

When I finally woke up, I sat up in the bed, looking around And Kumiko was still asleep so I just sat up there in bed, for a Moment, trying to figure out what had happened.

After stirring for a moment, kumiko sat up, looking around and just as mystified as me, she said," Where are we?'

I shrugged and said, "I honestly don't know."

A knock came to the door, and the taxi-drivers voice Boomed into the room, "You folks decent?"

We said yes, and he came in saying, "I hope you both had A Decent rest."

We assured him that we had, and he said, "I hope you can Forgive me for taking you to a place like I did last night. And you Can bet! That won't ever happen again."

I said, "We really appreciate what you've done for us and Really don't know what we can do to compensate you for Helping us."

The Taxi-driver smiled and said," Look! You're a black-man In an Air Force Uniform, and your wife is Asian. SO! That means That you've been in the Air Force for quite a spell."

I said, "Yes-sir!" He said, "Tell me, what brings you to Washington, D.C."

I explained my situation to him and he said, "No problem! I think we can get you straight real quick. I think I know where The Office you want is located, and after you've washed up and Eaten breakfast, I'll take you there.

After washing up, and eating a very big breakfast, he drove Us to an office complex and guided us to a building. Once inside The office, we could see that it was right on target and that we Were in the right place.

Once I stated my case, they assured me that I would be Re-assigned, and to look for new orders within the next week.

Once we were finished there, we stepped outside and the Cab-driver was right there waiting.

He took us back to his house, and left us there with his Family again, while he went off on his days-work.

That evening, he drove us to the Airport, where we got Tickets to fly home to Newark, New Jersey.

At the house, I took what money I had, and added the bit My wife had and when our benefactor came home, I sat down In the kitchen with him and presented the money to him.

I said, "It's not much, but it's all we've got right now. He looked at me, anger and resentment coming, and going From his eye in a breath and said," Look! I didn't do this for any Money. For all I know, you could be one of my son's out there Needing help.

Now what would it look like, if I charged my own son a fee For helping him?" Nodding his head, he shoved the money back At me, with a big hand saying, "I Don't think so!"

There were no words that I could think of, that could Express how I felt, when he said that.

When it was time for us to go to the Airport, the whole Family tagged along to see us off.

I never forgot that cab driver, although I never heard of or From him or his family again, I never forgot them, and never Will.

THE END

THE SLAMMER!

Out of all of my experiences, I actually spent ten days in Jail for trying to disciplining my eldest daughter.

Believe me, it was one ten day experience that I will never Forget.

How it occurred was, I was preparing to go to my job as Security Guard, at the Long Beach Naval Shipyard.

My eldest daughter Yolanda, had been acting up, and had Become some-what defiant in her attitude.

But! When they are 15 – 16 yrs. old, either you are going to guide them, or they are going to guide you. And believe me, I wasn't about to be the one, who was going to be guided.

That night, of all nights, she decided to bump heads with Me, and I wasn't having any of it.

We actually turned a shouting match into fist-ti-cuffs and Right away, my middle-son Estevan called the cops.

When they came, they separated us, and once they had us Separated, they began getting the story from both my ex-wife, Me, and the kids.

When all was said and done, I was placed under arrest but, Was allowed to go to work that night.

I was given a date to go To court, and had to move out of The house, and into a one Bedroom apartment.

I moved and worked up until I reached my court date, and When I went to court, I was given ten days in jail.

I was then taken from court to the city jail in handcuffs, Once there, the cuffs were removed and I was processed in, Given bedding, and assigned to an area.

In the almost suffocating heat, the glaring light's, and the Different foul Smells of the men and the cells, the noise of a Man relieving his bowels in one corner, into the one and only Toilet, the Predator's eyeing the newcomers, waiting to pounce On them and take whatever they had of value.

Talking, laughing, groan's, and pained calls, coughs, and Finally the smell of fear, a fear that made me warry of these Strangers, for surely in my mind, I thought that I had entered Into the doors of the true hell.

I was plunged into all of this chaos, where misdemeanors Were mixed with felons, and I was at risk of being violated.

Suddenly! A young, black, felon about 19 or 20, while I was In my sixties, approached me, his eyes on my sneakers,

He said loudly," I like those Shoe's!"

I said, just as loud, "Well! When you get out of here, Maybe you can buy yourself a pair."

Looking me straight in my eye's he said loudly," No! I don't Think you understand what I'm saying. So! Let's try that again! I LIKE THOSE SHOE'S! That means, that you take them off and GIVE! Them to me. NOW!"

I started to answer him, my anger getting the best of me, Because I knew that he was trying to bully me, and show his Dominance of an older man.

All talk had stopped, and all eyes were on me and the Young man. Just as I was going to return a flippant remark, he Rose two or three feet in the air and the look on his face made Me know that he was scared out of his wits, as he dangled There in mid-air. I looked past him and my eye's met the Biggest, most muscular Mexican, I had ever seen.

He said, as he stared at the now dangling young man, "You Messin with my Grandpa?"

And like an avenging angel, he shook the now frightened Young man, saying, as he turned to a now enthralled audience.

He said, "This could be YOU! So, if any of you have a beef With MY GRANPA!!! You bring it to me first! And if any of you, ANY OF YOU even touch him accidentally, you have to answer to me."

Looking around the crowded cell, he lowered the young Man to the floor, and we watched him scurry into a dim corner Of the huge cell, not to be heard from again.

As things became, business as usual. And until my last day In lock-up, I had no trouble from anyone.

The day that I was set free from lock-up, Ten days that Made me know, that I would never return to a place like that Ever again.

When I finally stepped out on the street, smelling pure, Sweet air, feeling the breeze upon my cheeks, watching as People went about their morning affairs, I felt uplifted and I Wanted to shout out that I was free.

I knew, as I hailed a taxi, that I would have some hard Choice's to make.

But! For that moment, I relished the two things that was Foremost, I was free and had choices.

The End

THE CHINESE COLLAR SHIRT

Out of all of my travels to foreign lands, I can never forget
The time that my brother and I were both stationed in Japan
together. Me, in Nagoya, Japan. Charles, in Hokaido, Japan,
as far north as you could get, at the same time, as luck Would
have it.

We were both in the Air Force, only joined at different
Times. Me first, then later Charles.

Anyway, Charles stayed for three days, and was a
Welcoming diversion for my wife Kumiko.

But! With that diversion, came a price. She took them on
The base and treated them to a small buying spree, buying
Them Clothes, and stuff from the BX.

By the time I got home from work, the damage had been
Done, but I didn't protest or say anything. So, after a few day's
More, Charles said that they would have to leave, because he
Had to get back to Hokaido and get to work.

So! The next morning, I said my goodbyes, before leaving
For work, while Kumiko helped them pack.

And pack they did, because when I got home after work, We were going to go on base to the movie and I had decided to Wear the brand new Chinese collared shirt, that one of my Buddies had given me, because it was too small for him, but fit Me just right.

I turned my shirt drawer upside down trying to find that Shirt but, it was no-where in the house.

So I had to choose another shirt but, I knew that shirts Don't just disappear into thin air.

During that whole evening out, I thought about the Missing shirt, and when we got home, I asked Kumiko about The shirt.

She said, "What is this about a shirt! Here you've got a closet full of shirts, and you're having fits about one shirt?" Nodding her head, she gave me a strange look, saying," Are You alright?"

I glared at her saying, "Yea! I'm fine."

But! I kept looking around for the next few days, without Bringing up the subject again.

But, that shirt wasn't far from my mind, as my mind turned To how the shirt could have possibly disappeared.

Suddenly, it dawned on me that Charles had come on his Sudden visit. And, suddenly I knew where my shirt had gone.

Either through a burst of generosity, Kumiko had packed The shirt in with his stuff, as he was packing to leave, or Charles Had stashed the shirt while he was packing.

Either way, I was still pretty mad about losing that shirt,
But! I never mentioned it to Charles but, for a very long time,
I held that against him.

And even today, I think about that shirt that I had, but
Never got the chance to wear.

The End

THE TIN LIZZIE

I guess it was about 1957-58, when I had been stationed at The Air Force Station, in Ocean City New Jersey, right outside Of Atlantic City.

Atlantic City of that period of time, was mostly Hotels, Celebrities, the Boardwalk, and Arcades.

The hotels booking the most famous celebrities of that Time period.

My wife and I were re-assigned to this base when I went to Washington D.C. and got my assignment changed.

It was a stroke of luck that we got assigned so close to Home, because, by being re-assigned in Ocean City NJ, At Palermo, AFS, we were a hop, step, and a jump away from My home town of Newark, NJ.

After being there for a while, I decided to try and get a job In one of the Hotels because, we could use the money.

I got an after-hours job in the Ambassador Hotel as a dish-Washer, in one of two huge kitchens.

And from 5PM, Until 1AM. I worked on a civilian job, discounting the time I had for a wife that I rarely saw.

My father had died maybe while I was stationed in Japan, But! As fortune would have it, I went to DC. And got my Assigned base changed to from one in Michigan to one in Ocean City, New Jersey, an Air Force Station right outside of Atlantic City, New Jersey, my wife and I lived in Atlantic City.

My mother called me asking if I could come home, and Move the car. It had been ticketed a few times, and she Couldn't afford the tickets, and she had no one to move it. I went to a couple of my friends, and asked them if they Would help me move the car, probably to a car lot down in Atlantic City.

I told my mother that I had gotten a couple of my buddies To help me move the car and that we would be up there the Next weekend to pick it up.

I wanted as many able-bodied men with me as I could Have along, just-in-case, there were problems that needed Solving.

It didn't seem to be a situation that couldn't be handled. All we had to do was get through the turnpike, onto the I-10 Freeway, and it was a straight shot from there to Atlantic City.

BUT! As fate would have it, we were not going to have Such an easy ride, as we thought.

We no-sooner got on the Turn-pike, than the damned car
Started smoking.

Belching out this odorous, oily, obnoxious cloud that hung
Over the car like some odorous beacon, telling the police,"
HEY! YOU GUY'S! WE'RE OVER HERE."

For a long stretch, we didn't run into any police cars but,
Before we got off of the Turnpike, we were stopped and yea!
Ticketed.

Every time we stopped, we checked to see where that oily
Smoke was coming from, only we could never find the source.

I cannot tell you the relief I felt, when we finally came up
On the off-ramp to Atlantic City.

That was when the car had its final break-down. After
About a half-hour of tinkering, we finally got the car moving
Again, and got to our final destination.

Once we finally parked the car, we checked out the motor,
And found that the reason the damned car had been smoking
So much, was because there were old rags that had ignited
and Had smoldered all the way from Newark to Atlantic City,
Without really catching on fire.

We parked the car on my street, and after going through
The want ads, we found a junkyard that would come to my
Street, and tow it away.

Once we finally parked the car, we checked out the motor,
And found that the reason the damned car had been smoking
So much, was because there were old oily rags that had ignited,
But only put out a black, oily, foul smelling smoke, (Sitting

right On the engine block) without catching fire, and had really Made our trip into a lot of fun.

But! I can truly say, that I felt that my father was probably There, even after he left had us.

The End

THE DEAN'S LIST

This incident occurred while my wife and I were both going to Junior College at East Los Angeles College.

I worked at the Veterans Administration in West Los Angeles, While living in East Los Angeles.

It was a hectic time for both of us because, Trini had to tend to The tykes we had at home, as well as the ones in school. And then After she picked up the ones in school, she had to drive all the way Out to West LA in all of that traffic and pick me up, and drive back Home, and this was five days a week.

Trini's mother or sister would come over our house and watch The kids while we were in school.

Our weekends were spent taking the kids to the park or to the Movies, or wherever.

After our first semester in school, we got our grades, and that night, Trini came home with a worried look on her face. I asked her What was the matter and she said, "I made the Dean's List."

I was shocked and said, (Only to make things worse),"
YyyyouMade the Dean's list? Oh! MAN! You really screwed
the pooch this Time! DAMNED!"

My outburst only made her cry harder. I finally got her
to stopCrying, saying," No Sweat! You can make it up next
semester."

We left it there, both feeling subdued by the news, and I
can only Guess that she was at her lowest point.

The next day, while I was at work, I said to one of my
friends, "Man! My wife really screwed up in school."

He said, "OK! So how did she screw up?"

I said, anger in my voice," She made the Dean's List!"
Looking my Friend in his eye, I said," Do you know what
that means?"

My friend frowned and said," Do YOU! Know what that
means?"

I said," No! I don't, but! I know it can't be anything good?"

My friend smiled and said," Good? Man! It's not just
good, it's Great! You should be proud of her. She made the
dean's list at the First try, even with all of those kids. Man!
That's the highest honor any One can get in college.

"Man! You should be proud of her, instead of Pissed-off!
Hell! She Did something in her first term that most people
can't do in a full term.

"The best I can say is, that you have one smart assed!
Wife, and Who knows, you can probably learn a lot from
her yourself!"

That afternoon, when my wife came to pick me up, I said, "Look! I owe you an apology."

She looked at me, a question in her eye's, saying, "An apology?

Why?"

I said," Because, both of us were wrong about the dean's list."

A perplexed look came to her face, as she maneuvered expertly Through the late afternoon (bumper to bumper) traffic.

She finally said, "What do you mean?"

I said," The Dean's list. Here we thought it was something wrong, Something that would mess you up, as far as your grade go. Well! It Turns out, that you maxed your exams, and got top grades in your class, Hell! I've got the smartest wife on the planet."

Giving me a dubious look, she said," Yea! OK!"

But, even though she made light of it, I noticed that her spirits Were lifted, and even though we didn't mention it again, I knew that She was as proud of herself as I was of her.

THE END

TUNNEL RAT

The Year was 1962, and I was stationed at Bangkok, Thailand, Working out of the shops area, on base. I ran a shop That in-compassed Return Veterans from the war zone, and Helped them with rest Area vocational interest's such as, Photography, Lapidary, Leather-craft, Etc.

On one of these day, after I had left my shop and had gone To the BX-Snack Bar for lunch, while I was eating my lunch, I Noticed an Army Ranger Major eyeballing me.

As I sat eating, he strolled over to my table and said, "Mind If I sit down?" I nodded, that it was alright if he sat down.

He looked to be a strapping 240-260 lbs. of muscle and Blood.

He was slightly scary because, his eyes were light blue, and it seemed to me, that they were cold and remote.

He said, "Can I ask you a question?

I nodded yes, and he said, "How tall are you?"

I said, "I'm 5'5" Tall. Why?"

He said, in a quiet voice, "You meet the most important Requirement, and you're a rare breed and can truly serve Your country."

After lunch, I went to the BX and was browsing the Different Aisle's, finally I bought a pack of cigarettes and left.

When I got back to my hooch, I was surprised to see that Very same officer sitting out front, drinking a beer, and smoking A cigarette.

When I asked him how he found out where I was, he said, "Oh! I asked around."

I said, "Sir! Exactly what do you want out of me?"

He said, "I have to leave in a couple of days, and I want to See if I can't get you to join my unit."

I said a bit angrily, "And what unit is that?"

He said, "It's a new concept, but! It's affective."

I said, "OK! So! What's this new concept?"

He said, a bit of a wicked smile on his face, "Well! We're Taking a lot of the shorter men, and turning them into more or Less, unsung heroes.

"Due to the fact that you're 5'5" tall, you fit the Dynamics Of what we call a tunnel rat.

"What happens, is that you guys go into the tunnels that the VC have dug, and blow them to hell and back.

"You're their size, and can fit comfortably in their tunnels, So you go in plant bombs and get out quick."

Looking at me with those unfeeling eyes, he said," So! What do you think? Can you hack what I just told you?"

I said, "Sir! I've got a job already, and I think it's pretty Important. I help rehab the guy's that return from in-country, And come to Ubon Thailand, for a little R&R."

"I think that's just as important as putting my life on the Line, by going into a tunnel, and getting myself blown up, or Getting myself killed in some other way."

Waving away my objections, he said, "True! Your job here Is commendable, and as is all the jobs here, it's one of true Important's, But! It doesn't hold a candle to what you could do To save lives, and stop the enemy from having arms, money, Food, and the energy to put up a fight.

"Once they realize that we have the means to fight their Fire, with the same fire, and that we can destroy their efforts, By beating them at their own game. They will have to resort to Other means. But! We'll have shown them that we are Willing to use their tactics against them and win."

"You can be a part of us winning by showing them that we Also have the means to use their methods against them."

Looking at his watch, he said," Look! I have to go, but I'll Be back in about a week. I'll be stopping by and checking with You again.

"I want you to think about this seriously, and when I Return, I want to be able to assign you to my unit."

Shaking my hand, he said," I'll be seeing you soon!" And he Was gone.

I was near the end of my tour of duty and would be going Back to the states in months and had my reasons all lined up, so That, when I saw the Major again, I could explain them to him.

But, I never saw the Major again, even though I always Kept my sights out to see him.

I never knew what happened to him and every once in a While I Think about him and wonder what happened to him.

Did he get killed by the Viet Cong? Did he die in some Other way? This I will never know, but I will never forget him, Even though the year is 2015, and I'm in my 80's, I'll never Forget him.

The End

NEIGHBORHOOD WATCH

I was born, 20 August, 1933, the second son, of the Bateman Family in the City Hospital, in the City of Newark, New Jersey. I was raised in the Third Ward Newark, which was an All black neighborhood.

You see! Newark was divided into wards. Although The Third Ward was all black, when it came to work, the venders Scattered and went to all of the different wards. At night, every-One would go back to their own wards, where their homes were.

In our neighborhood, we had the Thirteenth Precinct Better known as the Police Department.

The difference in the Police Departments of 30's, and 40's, and the Police Departments of today, are vastly, and Absolutely different.

The Police Officers of the 30's and 40's, watched over The ward they were assigned to, But! Left the handling of the Children to the parents.

It must have been a pretty good method, because there was Less crime's in the city, and most if not all of the children Were always in school because, they all had to confront their Mothers, if they cut school.

And they didn't want to do that, because no excuse would Keep them from having their rear-end's busted. And believe me, The mother's in those days, knew how to bust backsides.

In those days, even the criminals respected the neighborhood Watch, which turned out to be all of the mothers in the Neighborhood.

The few burglaries that they had, were far and in between Because, if they were caught, the police would really give them Something to think about. And once it was known, throughout the neighborhood, that a Member of the community was the culprit, sneaking and stealing From them, they would either move, or try to appease the families By remuneration, or some type of payback.

Back in the day, there weren't any guns that looked real, or Guns that could shoot any types of bullets, except they would Make popping noises, and sometimes used caps that made popping Sounds. So! You couldn't simulate a true gunfight. The guns they Had were absolutely fake.

When I was about 15 years old, I begged my father to get me A Red Ryder B-B-Gun. He said alright, I could have a Red Ryder B-B-Gun, But! it would have to come out of my own wages. (I was working in Sam's Grocery store at the time.)

So! After saving up the money out of my weekly $5.00 a Week wages, the rifle costing $25.00 Dollars, I had enough saved to Buy The B-B-Gun.

My mom had me fill out the paperwork to send for the B-B-Gun, and when she went to the store, she mail the letter and the $25.00 for the B-B-Gun.

To show you that all kids think the same, when the B-B-Gun Finally came, and I finally had the Red Ryder B-B-Gun in my Hands, I immediately became destructive.

I went out on the back porch, and wanting to tryout the B-B-Gun, I started to sniping people as they walked down and up the Street.

After shooting at a few people, and seeing some of them Flinch as a few of the BB's found their mark, I sat back and Relaxed, and when I started to go on a second round of shooting, I felt a presence behind me.

Turning my head to look behind me, I saw that my father was Standing in the doorway, and boy! Was he mad!

He said, his voice heavy with anger, "I see that as soon as you got that damned gun, you put it to good use.

Dreading the coming moments, I said," I'm sorry dad, it Won't happen again."

My dad smiled saying, "True! I'm sure it won't happen Again!"

Looking me dead in my eyes, he said," It won't happen Again, because you just lost the privilege of having it."

He held out his hand, a smile on his face, as I placed the B-B-Rifle in his hands.

Weighing the rifle in his hands, holding it by its barrel, he Swung it, and slammed the stock on the top step, and broke it off Leaving the bare metal in one hand.

Taking the barrel near the muzzle, and on the end near where The stock use to be, he bent it into a bow, and handing it back to Me, he said," Now! Try shooting at people with this.

He never busted my backside once, but broke my heart by Breaking the Rifle into pieces. We never spoke of the rifle again And I never got another gun after that, nor have I ever owned a gun, of Any type.

THE END

SLEEPERS

Ahmed sat on the stoop, gazing off into the distance, looking around the Neighborhood where he had been born.

The corner Bodega, where the loud speakers over the doorway entering it, were blaring an olio of music, some jazz, some rap, and Some music from Iran.

Ahmed sat there trying to make sense of what his brothers actions of the past few weeks signified.

This was his neighborhood, which was nearly all Arab and although he understood the language, he never thought about speaking it that much because, being born and reared in the United States, his first language was English, although he had to maintain a certain amount of Iranian in order to communicate with his mother and father who, although they had learned a smatter, of English, spoke mostly Iranian, so that like most of the people living in the neighborhood they wanted to keep the children's natural language alive to them.

Although his brother Sahir was only three years older than him, it rankled him that he was treated like a child, after all, he was fifteen but, already he felt like he was able to take care of himself.

Sahir was eighteen and was always guarding him every-since 9/11 and the destruction of the Twin Towers. Their neighborhood was always tense with a cord of fear snaking through it, drawing the people closer together.

Their parents had been killed in a horrific car accident, which was the fault of a drunk driver on an ordinary night, when they were driving home from the Bordega the boy's father managed.

The Bordega was owned by a white man, whose name was Dana Pritchard, a man who owned many buildings in their neighborhood.

The night of the accident, Ahmed's brother Sahir said to him, as they lay in their beds, "I hate these people."

Ahmed said, "Why? They didn't do anything to us."

Sahir said angrily, "Little brother, you have a lot to learn about Americans. You are still too young to appreciate that we are only being catered to by these people."

Ahmed said, a puzzled note in his voice, "What has happened to you Sahir? Why are you so angry? So bitter??"

Sahir said, "Because after those airplanes crashed into the Towers and brought them down, right away, people from outside of this community began looking at all of us, like it was our fault."

He was silent for a moment before he continued by saying, "Remember when our uncle and aunt took us into their house after mom and dad were killed?"

Ahmed said, nodding in the dark, "Yes! And it was a very nice gesture. We were very lucky to have such wonderful kinfolk."

Sahir said, "They are more than wonderful, for they feel the same way I do.

"Ahmed was silent for a moment and then he said, "Exactly what do you mean, they think the same way you do?"

Sahir said, abruptly changing the subject," What do you think of our home-land Iran?" Ahmed said, a bit perplexed, "What homeland? I know that there's such a place but, I don't have any particular feelings, or think anything about Iran. In my history class, we've discussed Iran, but heck! It's like talking about something out of the Thief of Bagdad, or the Arabian Nights or something Besides, this is where we were born, and this is probably where we'll die."

Sahir said, "I have been talking to uncle Faisal, and he said that even though they have been in this country for twenty years, and all of their children had been born here, they still longed to be back in our homeland of Iran."

Losing his patience Ahmid said, "SAHID! You will stop calling Iran, our Country!! You were not born there, and I was not born there. We were born in this country, and grew up in a brownstone in Brooklyn, New York and that has been our home for all of our lives, at least up to now."

Sahid said, "True! I agree and . . . .!"

Ahmid said abruptly, "So why are you now saying that Iran is our homeland? After all, the closest we have ever come to knowing this country, are by pictures from school books and Photo Albums, or once and a while on TV, and, from what I saw, I don't think I'd want to live among a lot of foreigners anyway."

Looking at his stunned brothers face, he continued speaking in the pregnant silence,"

We can speak the language and although I know everything that's going on, I'd rather stay here with my friends and all of the people I know."

Suddenly, Sahid said angrily," You actually love this country don't you? you don't see that we don't really fit in here. You know that whites look down on us, and we'll always live one step below the blacks, who also look down on us? Hell! Even the Asian's act, like their superior to us.

But! in Iran, we will have a chance to be among our own kind without having to answer to so many people who consider us inferior."

Ahmid said tentatively, "You've been talking to our uncle and aunt again." Sighing deeply he continued, "They tried to convince me too but, I guess they got frustrated because, they stopped trying to talk to me about it. I guess they decided to get you to talk to me. " The last said with a trace Of impatience in his voice.

Sahid shrugging said," You don't understand and are still a boy. But when you are as old as I am, you will understand everything better."

Ahmid said, half serious, half-jokingly, Listen to you! You speak like you're an old man yet, you're only three years older than me."

One night, the boy's uncle and aunt explained to the boys their mission in America. Their uncle said,"

"We love you boys very much, and would not want anything bad to happen to either of you. But! we must explain, that for the last twenty years, we have been the part of a cell living in this country. We. . . .!"

Ahmid said," Like a jail cell or something?"

Uncle Fasil gave the boy an uncomfortable look but continued by saying, "We have established ourselves as working class people and own our Bordega. But soon, we will have to rise up and do the bidding of Allah."

Ahmid said, a note of awe mixed with anger in his voice," You mean that after being here for twenty years, you are going to do something terrible to these people? These people! Blacks, Whites, and Asians, ho have been our friends. People I have seen you eat and drink with People who's children, I have played with, and have known all of my life." Looking impatient, he said angrily, "Why are you doing this?"

Uncle Fasil said gruffly, "It was business, just business."

Hamid said, "But you have been free all of these years, free to run your business, free to have lots of money in the bank, and live in a fine apartment." The tone in his voice had become strident and bitter as he continued. "You have been doing every-thing American for all of these years, and now you would do something terrible to end all that my brother and I have ever known by wanting us to join you in this madness?"

Uncle Fasil exchanged a look with his wife, and after a pause he said, "Yes! As crazy as it might sound, we made a pact with Alqueda many years ago, now we have been summoned to the fore-front to fulfill that pact. So! in the name of allah, and the cause, we will serve to the very death."

Looking at his wife he said, "We were hoping that you boys would serve with us."

Sahid said, "1 would gladly help you, if it ment that my brother and I could live without feeling that we are being watched all of the time."

Their aunt said, Looking directly into Ahmid's eyes," And you Ahmid? What about you?"

Ahmid shrugged saying, "I do not understand. Sure! We are being Watched but! I guess we would be watching them twice as hard, if any of them came into our neighborhood and killed some of our young men and women.

But this? I don't know. Being born here? Learning about the many things I've learned, not having to worship other than Allah, while they have many different faiths in this Country. Going to school with different races of children and learning about their different lives, being able to come and go as we please, any time day or night."

Feeling uncomfortable under the three sets of eyes that stared at him, and he felt more uncomfortable as he fumble for words.

His uncle glared at him saying, "And this is what you think? This is all that you have been taught by your parents? To fall victim to the soft life Of these Americans? To become just as corrupt as they are?"

Ahmid, not expecting such angry words from his uncle, became afraid and looking to his brother for support and protection, but Sahid was sitting across from him, a smirk on his face. He finally said, "Ahmid, You must listen to our uncle and aunt after all, they are our elders, and know what's best for us.

Ahmid said, a perplexed look on his face," But just as we have been living among these people as their neighbors, we have learned our countries language and have read the Koran and been to prayer.

I never found anywhere in that book that says that we must do terrible things to the people we have known all of our lives. Especially the ones that we have met that are outside of our neighborhood.

The Koran speaks of love and giving of ourselves openly. Not of sneaking around being Assissins, for people that are using us for their own selfish purposes. Besides, these people that plot and scheme, hate Americans with a passion and want to bring them down in any way they can. And I don't think I can be a part of that."

Sahid said, Looking at his Uncle and Aunt, "I never thought I would hear a brother of mine spout the garbage that these Infidels have brain washed him with."

Looking at his uncle and aunt with intense anger in his eyes, he said, "You have not done a very good job of teaching Ahmid that we must stand with the people of our country, and not with these people that are so corrupt that they murder and kill their own for any reason under the sun." Looking at his brother he said, as though he were speaking to a stranger, "What can I do to change your mind about what role we are going to play in this war we are in?"

Ahmid shrugged and yawned widely and said, looking at his uncle, "It is late, and tomorrow is a school day. I will sleep on what I have heard and give you my answer tomorrow night."

That night as he lay in his bed, he thought to himself,' I can't deal with this. My own brother trying to make me join something that is against all that I have learned to believe in. Heck! I'm not mad at any of my friends, and I have lot of friends in school of all colors and races.' Glaring up into the darkness he thought,' But what can I do? Tomorrow night they will only be at me again to join them.'

Suddenly, he had a thought and, a jolt of fear and excitement raced through him. Settling down he thought to himself,' We have relatives in Long Island. Relatives who

I'm pretty sure, live the life they love, and love the life they live and I'm sure they don't' want to give that life up. Now just maybe, if I can get their phone number, I can get them to agree to let me come there and stay.' With fear and doubt flooding his mind, he quietly got out of bed and taking down his small suitcase as quiet as he could, he packed his meager belongings.

Tiptoeing through the dark apartment, where everyone else was asleep, he went quietly to his uncles desk and turning on the desk lamp, he picked up his uncles rolodex, thumbing through it, he came to his cousins address and phone number. He quickly wrote the information down and picking up his suitcase, he turned out the desk lamp and continued tiptoeing to the front door. Opening the front door quietly, he stood there for a moment more, then he was gone.

Reaching his cousins house via train connections, he stood before her door, not sure of how he was feeling or how she would re-act to his being there so early in the morning, He took a deep breath and knocked on the door, his heart in his mouth. After a few minutes, the lights went on inside the house and over the door which was opened by my cousin The next day, Ahmid disappeared from the neighborhood and was never heard from again.

THE END

Printed in the United States
By Bookmasters